Stories of
Red Hanrahan

W. B. Yeats

Contents

STORIES OF
RED HANRAHAN

BY

W. B. Yeats

I owe thanks to Lady Gregory,
who helped me to rewrite
The Stories of Red Hanrahan
in the beautiful country speech of Kiltartan,
and nearer to the tradition of the people among
whom he, or some likeness of him, drifted and is remembered.

RED HANRAHAN.

anrahan, the hedge schoolmaster, a tall, strong, red-haired young man, came into the barn where some of the men of the village were sitting on Samhain Eve. It had been a dwelling-house, and when the man that owned it had built a better one, he had put the two rooms together, and kept it for a place to store one thing or another. There was a fire on the old hearth, and there were dip candles stuck in bottles, and there was a black quart bottle upon some boards that had been put across two barrels to make a table. Most of the men were sitting beside the fire, and one of them was singing a long wandering song, about a Munster man and a Connaught man that were quarrelling about their two provinces.

Hanrahan went to the man of the house and said, 'I got your message'; but when he had said that, he stopped, for an old mountainy man that had a shirt and trousers of unbleached flannel, and that was sitting by himself near the door, was looking at him, and moving an old pack of cards about in his hands and muttering. 'Don't mind him,' said the man of the house; 'he is only some stranger came in awhile ago, and we bade him welcome, it being Samhain night, but I think he is not in his right wits. Listen to him now and you will hear what he is saying.'

They listened then, and they could hear the old man muttering to himself as he turned the cards, 'Spades and Diamonds, Courage and Power; Clubs and Hearts, Knowledge and Pleasure.'

'That is the kind of talk he has been going on with for the last hour,' said the man of the house, and Hanrahan turned his eyes from the old man as if he did not like to be looking at him.

'I got your message,' Hanrahan said then; '"he is in the barn with his three first cousins from Kilchriest," the messenger said, "and there are some of the neighbours with them.'"

'It is my cousin over there is wanting to see you,' said the man of the house, and he called over a young frieze-coated man, who was listening to the song, and said, 'This is Red Hanrahan you have the message for.'

'It is a kind message, indeed,' said the young man, 'for it comes from your sweetheart, Mary Lavelle.'

'How would you get a message from her, and what do you know of her?'

'I don't know her, indeed, but I was in Loughrea yesterday, and a neighbour of hers that had some dealings with me was saying that she bade him send you word, if he met any one from this side in the market, that her mother has died from her, and if you have a mind yet to join with herself, she is willing to keep her word to you.'

'I will go to her indeed,' said Hanrahan.

'And she bade you make no delay, for if she has not a man in the house before the month is out, it is likely the little bit of land will be given to another.'

When Hanrahan heard that, he rose up from the bench he had sat down on. 'I will make no delay indeed,' he said, 'there is a full moon, and if I get as far as Gilchreist to-night, I will reach to her before the setting of the sun to-morrow.'

When the others heard that, they began to laugh at him for being in such haste to go to his sweetheart, and one asked him if he would leave his school in the old lime-kiln, where he was giving the children such good learning. But he said the children would be glad enough in the morning to find the place empty, and no one to keep them at their task; and as for his school he could set it up again in any place, having as he had his little inkpot hanging from his neck by a chain, and his big Virgil and his primer in the skirt of his coat.

Some of them asked him to drink a glass before he went, and a young man caught hold of his coat, and said he must not leave them without singing the song he had made in praise of Venus and of Mary Lavelle. He drank a glass of whiskey, but he said he would not stop but would set out on his journey.

'There's time enough, Red Hanrahan,' said the man of the house. 'It will be time enough for you to give up sport when you are after your marriage, and it might be a long time before we will see you again.'

'I will not stop,' said Hanrahan; 'my mind would be on the roads all the time, bringing me to the woman that sent for me, and she lonesome and watching till I come.'

Some of the others came about him, pressing him that had been such a pleasant comrade, so full of songs and every kind of trick and fun, not to leave them till the night would be over, but he refused them all, and shook them off, and went to the door. But as he put his foot over the threshold, the strange old man stood up and put his hand that was thin and withered like a bird's claw on Hanrahan's hand, and said: 'It is not Hanrahan, the learned man and the great songmaker, that should go out from a gathering like this, on a Samhain night. And stop here, now,' he said, 'and play a hand with me; and here is an old pack of cards has done its work many a night before this, and old as it is, there has been much of the riches of the world lost and won over it.'

One of the young men said, 'It isn't much of the riches of the world has stopped with yourself, old man,' and he looked at the old man's bare feet, and they all laughed. But Hanrahan did not laugh, but he sat down very quietly, without a word. Then one of them said, 'So you will stop with us after all, Hanrahan'; and the old man said: 'He will stop indeed, did you not hear me asking him?'

They all looked at the old man then as if wondering where he came from. 'It is far I am come,' he said, 'through France I have come, and through Spain, and by Lough Greine of the hidden mouth, and none has refused me anything.' And then he was silent and nobody liked to question him, and they began to play. There were six men at the boards playing, and the others were looking on behind. They played two or three games for nothing, and then the old man took a fourpenny bit, worn very thin and smooth, out from his pocket, and he called to the rest to put something on the game. Then they all put down something on the boards, and little as it was it looked much, from the way it was shoved from one to another, first one man winning it and then his neighbour. And some-times the luck would go against a man and he would have nothing left, and then one or another would lend him something, and he would pay it again out of his winnings, for neither good nor bad luck stopped long with anyone.

And once Hanrahan said as a man would say in a dream, 'It is time for me to be going the road'; but just then a good card came to him, and he played it out, and all the money began to come to him. And once he thought of Mary Lavelle, and he sighed; and that time his luck went from him, and he forgot her again.

But at last the luck went to the old man and it stayed with him, and all they had flowed into him, and he began to laugh little laughs to himself, and to sing over and over to himself, 'Spades and Diamonds, Courage and Power,' and so on, as if it was a verse of a song.

And after a while anyone looking at the men, and seeing the way their bodies were rocking to and fro, and the way they kept their eyes on the old man's hands, would think they had drink taken, or that the whole store they had in the world was put on the cards; but that was not so, for the quart bottle had not been disturbed since the game began, and was nearly full yet, and all that was on the game was a few sixpenny bits and shillings, and maybe a handful of coppers.

'You are good men to win and good men to lose,' said the old man, 'you have play in your hearts.' He began then to shuffle the cards and to mix them, very quick and fast, till at last they could not see them to be cards at all, but you would think him to be making rings of fire in the air, as little lads would make them with whirling a lighted stick; and after that it seemed to them that all the room was dark, and they could see nothing but his hands and the cards.

And all in a minute a hare made a leap out from between his hands, and whether it was one of the cards that took that shape, or whether it was made out of nothing in the palms of his hands, nobody knew, but there it was running on the floor of the barn, as quick as any hare that ever lived.

Some looked at the hare, but more kept their eyes on the old man, and while they were looking at him a hound made a leap out between his hands, the same way as the hare did, and after that another hound and another, till there was a whole pack of them following the hare round and round the barn.

The players were all standing up now, with their backs to the boards, shrinking from the hounds, and nearly deafened with the noise of their yelping, but as quick as the hounds were they could not overtake the hare, but it went round, till at the last it seemed as if a blast of wind burst open the barn door, and the hare doubled and made a leap over the boards where the men had been playing, and went out of the door and away through the night, and the hounds over the boards and through the door after it.

Then the old man called out, 'Follow the hounds, follow the hounds, and it is a great hunt you will see to-night,' and he went out after them. But used as the men were to go hunting after hares, and ready as they were for any sport, they were in dread to go out into the night, and it was only Hanrahan that rose up and that said, 'I will follow, I will follow on.'

'You had best stop here, Hanrahan,' the young man that was nearest him said, 'for you might be going into some great danger.' But Hanrahan said, 'I will see fair play, I will see fair play,' and he went stumbling out of the door like a man in a dream, and the door shut after him as he went.

He thought he saw the old man in front of him, but it was only his own shadow that the full moon cast on the road before him, but he could hear the hounds crying after the hare over the wide green fields of Granagh, and he followed them very fast for there was nothing to stop him; and after a while he came to smaller fields that had little walls of loose stones around them, and he threw the stones down as he crossed them, and did not wait to put them up again; and he passed by the place where the river goes under ground at Ballylee, and he could hear the hounds going before him up towards the head of the river. Soon he found it harder to run, for it was uphill he was going, and clouds came over the moon, and it was hard for him to see his way, and once he left the path to take a short cut, but his foot slipped into a boghole and he had to come back to it. And how long he was going he did not know, or what way he went, but at last he was up on the bare mountain, with nothing but the rough heather about him, and he could neither hear the hounds nor any other thing. But their cry began to come to him again, at first far off and then very near, and when it came quite close to him, it went up all of a sudden into the air, and there was the sound of hunting over his head; then it went away northward till he could hear nothing more at all. 'That's not fair,' he said, 'that's not fair.' And he could walk no longer, but sat down on the heather where he was, in the heart of Slieve Echtge, for all the strength had gone from him, with the dint of the long journey he had made.

And after a while he took notice that there was a door close to him, and a light coming from it, and he wondered that being so close to him he had not seen it before. And he rose up, and tired as he was he went in at the door, of and although it was night time outside, it was daylight he found within. And presently he met with an old man that had been gathering summer thyme and yellow flag-flowers, and it seemed as if all the sweet smells of the summer were with them. And the old man said: 'It is a long time you have been coming to us, Hanrahan the learned man and the great songmaker.'

And with that he brought him into a very big shining house, and every grand thing Hanrahan had ever heard of, and every colour he had ever seen, were in it. There was a high place at the end of the house, and on it there was sitting in a high chair a woman, the most beautiful the world ever saw, having a long pale face and flowers about it, but she had the tired look of one that had been long waiting. And there was sitting on the step below her chair four grey old women, and the one of them was holding a great cauldron in her lap; and another a great stone on her knees, and heavy as it was it seemed light to her; and another of them had a very long spear that was made of pointed wood; and the last of them had a sword that was without a scabbard. Red Hanrahan stood looking at them for a long Hanrahan-time, but none of them spoke any word to him or looked at him at all. And he had it in his mind to ask who that woman in the chair was, that was like a queen, and what she was waiting for; but ready as he was with his tongue and afraid of no person, he was in dread now to speak to so beautiful a woman, and in so grand a place. And then he thought to ask what were the four things the four grey old women were holding like great treasures, but he could not think of the right words to bring out.

Then the first of the old women rose up, holding the cauldron between her two hands, and she said 'Pleasure,' and Hanrahan said no word. Then the second old woman rose up with the stone in her hands, and she said 'Power'; and the third old woman rose up with the spear in her hand, and she said 'Courage'; and the last of the old women rose up having the sword in her hands, and she said 'Knowledge.' And everyone, after she had spoken, waited as if for Hanrahan to question her, but he said nothing at all. And then the four old women went out of the door, bringing their tour treasures with them, and as they went out one of them said, 'He has no wish for us'; and another said, 'He is weak, he is weak'; and another said, 'He is afraid'; and the last said, 'His wits are gone from him.' And then they all said 'Echtge, daughter of the Silver Hand, must stay in her sleep. It is a pity, it is a great pity.'

And then the woman that was like a queen gave a very sad sigh, and it seemed to Hanrahan as if the sigh had the sound in it of hidden streams; and if the place he was in had been ten times grander and more shining than it was, he could not have hindered sleep from coming on him; and he staggered like a drunken man and lay down there and then.

When Hanrahan awoke, the sun was shining on his face, but there was white frost on the grass around him, and there was ice on the edge of the stream he was lying by, and that goes running on through Daire- caol and Druim-da-rod. He knew by the shape of the hills and by the shining of Lough Greine in the distance that he was upon one of the hills of Slieve Echtge, but he was not sure how he came there; for all that had happened in the barn had gone from him, and all of his journey but the soreness of his feet and the stiffness in his bones.

It was a year after that, there were men of the village of Cappaghtagle sitting by the fire in a house on the roadside, and Red Hanrahan that was now very thin and worn and his hair very long and wild, came to the half-door and asked leave to come in and rest himself; and they bid him welcome because it was Samhain night. He sat down with them, and they gave him a glass of whiskey out of a quart bottle; and they saw the little inkpot hanging about his neck, and knew he was a scholar, and asked for stories about the Greeks.

He took the Virgil out of the big pocket of his coat, but the cover was very black and swollen with the wet, and the page when he opened it was very yellow, but that was no great matter, for he looked at it like a man that had never learned to read. Some young man that was there began to laugh at him then, and to ask why did he carry so heavy a book with him when he was not able to read it.

It vexed Hanrahan to hear that, and he put the Virgil back in his pocket and asked if they had a pack of cards among them, for cards were better than books. When they brought out the cards he took them and began to shuffle them, and while he was shuffling them something seemed to come into his mind, and he put his hand to his face like one that is trying to remember, and he said: 'Was I ever here before, or where was I on a night like this?' and then of a sudden he stood up and let the cards fall to the floor, and he said, 'Who was it brought me a message from Mary Lavelle?'

'We never saw you before now, and we never heard of Mary Lavelle,' said the man of the house. 'And who is she,' he said, 'and what is it you are talking about?'

'It was this night a year ago, I was in a barn, and there were men playing cards, and there was money on the table, they were pushing it from one to another here and there--and I got a message, and I was going out of the door to look for my sweetheart that wanted me, Mary Lavelle.' And then Hanrahan called out very loud: 'Where have I been since then? Where was I for the whole year?'

'It is hard to say where you might have been in that time,' said the oldest of the men, 'or what part of the world you may have travelled; and it is like enough you have the dust of many roads on your feet; for there are many go wandering and forgetting like that,' he said, 'when once they have been given the touch.'

'That is true,' said another of the men. 'I knew a woman went wandering like that through the length of seven years; she came back after, and she told her friends she had often been glad enough to eat the food that was put in the pig's trough. And it is best for you to go to the priest now,' he said, 'and let him take off you whatever may have been put upon you.'

'It is to my sweetheart I will go, to Mary Lavelle,' said Hanrahan; 'it is too long I have delayed, how do I know what might have happened her in the length of a year?'

He was going out of the door then, but they all told him it was best for him to stop the night, and to get strength for the journey; and indeed he wanted that, for he was very weak, and when they gave him food he eat it like a man that had never seen food before, and one of them said, 'He is eating as if he had trodden on the hungry grass.' It was in the white light of the morning he set out, and the time seemed long to him till he could get to Mary Lavelle's house. But when he came to it, he found the door broken, and the thatch dropping from the roof, and no living person to be seen. And when he asked the neighbours what had happened her, all they could say was that she had been put out of the house, and had married some labouring man, and they had gone looking for work to London or Liverpool or some big place. And whether she found a worse place or a better he never knew, but anyway he never met with her or with news of her again.

THE TWISTING OF THE ROPE.

anrahan was walking the roads one time near Kinvara at the fall of day, and he heard the sound of a fiddle from a house a little way off the road-side. He turned up the path to it, for he never had the habit of passing by any place where there was music or dancing or good company, without going in. The man of the house was standing at the door, and when Hanrahan came near he knew him and he said: 'A welcome before you, Hanrahan, you have been lost to us this long time.' But the woman of the house came to the door and she said to her husband: 'I would be as well pleased for Hanrahan not to come in to-night, for he has no good name now among the priests, or with women that mind them-selves, and I wouldn't wonder from his walk if he has a drop of drink taken.' But the man said, 'I will never turn away Hanrahan of the poets from my door,' and with that he bade him enter.

There were a good many neighbours gathered in the house, and some of them remembered Hanrahan; but some of the little lads that were in the corners had only heard of him, and they stood up to have a view of him, and one of them said: 'Is not that Hanrahan that had the school, and that was brought away by Them?' But his mother put her hand over his mouth and bade him be quiet, and not be saying things like that. 'For Hanrahan is apt to grow wicked,' she said, 'if he hears talk of that story, or if anyone goes questioning him.' One or another called out then, ask-ing him for a song, but the man of the house said it was no time to ask him for a song, before he had rested himself; and he gave him whiskey in a glass, and Hanra-han thanked him and wished him good health and drank it off.

The fiddler was tuning his fiddle for another dance, and the man of the house said to the young men, they would all know what dancing was like when they saw Hanrahan dance, for the like of it had never been seen since he was there before.

Hanrahan said he would not dance, he had better use for his feet now, travelling as he was through the five provinces of Ireland. Just as he said that, there came in at the half-door Oona, the daughter of the house, having a few bits of bog deal from Connemara in her arms for the fire. She threw them on the hearth and the flame rose up, and showed her to be very comely and smiling, and two or three of the young men rose up and asked for a dance. But Hanrahan crossed the floor and brushed the others away, and said it was with him she must dance, after the long road he had travelled before he came to her. And it is likely he said some soft word in her ear, for she said nothing against it, and stood out with him, and there were little blushes in her cheeks. Then other couples stood up, but when the dance was going to begin, Hanrahan chanced to look down, and he took notice of his boots that were worn and broken, and the ragged grey socks showing through them; and he said angrily it was a bad floor, and the music no great things, and he sat down in the dark place beside the hearth. But if he did, the girl sat down there with him.

The dancing went on, and when that dance was over another was called for, and no one took much notice of Oona and Red Hanrahan for a while, in the corner where they were. But the mother grew to be uneasy, and she called to Oona to come and help her to set the table in the inner room. But Oona that had never refused her before, said she would come soon, but not yet, for she was listening to whatever he was saying in her ear. The mother grew yet more uneasy then, and she would come nearer them, and let on to be stirring the fire or sweeping the hearth, and she would listen for a minute to hear what the poet was saying to her child. And one time she heard him telling about white-handed Deirdre, and how she brought the sons of Usnach to their death; and how the blush in her cheeks was not so red as the blood of kings' sons that was shed for her, and her sorrows had never gone out of mind; and he said it was maybe the memory of her that made the cry of the plover on the bog as sorrowful in the ear of the poets as the keening of young men for a comrade. And there would never have been that memory of her, he said, if it was not for the poets that had put her beauty in their songs. And the next time she did not well understand what he was saying, but as far as she could hear, it had the sound of poetry though it was not rhymed, and this is what she heard him say: 'The sun and the moon are the man and the girl, they are my life and your life, they are travelling and ever travelling through the skies as if under the one hood. It was God made them for one another. He made your life and my life before the beginning of the world, he made them that they might go through the world, up and down, like the two best dancers that go on with the dance up and down the long floor of the barn, fresh and laughing, when all the rest are tired out and leaning against the wall.'

The old woman went then to where her husband was playing cards, but he would take no notice of her, and then she went to a woman of the neighbours and said: 'Is there no way we can get them from one another?' and without waiting for an answer she said to some young men that were talking together: 'What good are you when you cannot make the best girl in the house come out and dance with you? And go now the whole of you,' she said, 'and see can you bring her away from the poet's talk.' But Oona would not listen to any of them, but only moved her hand as if to send them away. Then they called to Hanrahan and said he had best dance with the girl himself, or let her dance with one of them. When Hanrahan heard what they were saying he said: 'That is so, I will dance with her; there is no man in the house must dance with her but myself.'

He stood up with her then, and led her out by the hand, and some of the young men were vexed, and some began mocking at his ragged coat and his broken boots. But he took no notice, and Oona took no notice, but they looked at one another as if all the world belonged to themselves alone. But another couple that had been sitting together like lovers stood out on the floor at the same time, holding one another's hands and moving their feet to keep time with the music. But Hanrahan turned his back on them as if angry, and in place of dancing he began to sing, and as he sang he held her hand, and his voice grew louder, and the mocking of the young men stopped, and the fiddle stopped, and there was nothing heard but his voice that had in it the sound of the wind. And what he sang was a song he had heard or had made one time in his wanderings on Slieve Echtge, and the words of it as they can be put into English were like this:

O Death's old bony finger
Will never find us there
In the high hollow townland
Where love's to give and to spare;
Where boughs have fruit and blossom

At all times of the year;
Where rivers are running over
With red beer and brown beer.
An old man plays the bagpipes
In a gold and silver wood;
Queens, their eyes blue like the ice,
Are dancing in a crowd.

And while he was singing it Oona moved nearer to him, and the colour had gone from her cheek, and her eyes were not blue now, but grey with the tears that were in them, and anyone that saw her would have thought she was ready to follow him there and then from the west to the east of the world.

But one of the young men called out: 'Where is that country he is singing about? Mind yourself, Oona, it is a long way off, you might be a long time on the road before you would reach to it.' And another said: 'It is not to the Country of the Young you will be going if you go with him, but to Mayo of the bogs.' Oona looked at him then as if she would question him, but he raised her hand in his hand, and called out between singing and shouting: 'It is very near us that country is, it is on every side; it may be on the bare hill behind it is, or it may be in the heart of the wood.' And he said out very loud and clear: 'In the heart of the wood; oh, death will never find us in the heart of the wood. And will you come with me there, Oona?' he said.

But while he was saying this the two old women had gone outside the door, and Oona's mother was crying, and she said: 'He has put an enchantment on Oona. Can we not get the men to put him out of the house?'

'That is a thing you cannot do, said the other woman,' for he is a poet of the Gael, and you know well if you would put a poet of the Gael out of the house, he would put a curse on you that would wither the corn in the fields and dry up the milk of the cows, if it had to hang in the air seven years.'

'God help us,' said the mother, 'and why did I ever let him into the house at all, and the wild name he has!'

'It would have been no harm at all to have kept him outside, but there would great harm come upon you if you put him out by force. But listen to the plan I have to get him out of the house by his own doing, without anyone putting him from it at all.'

It was not long after that the two women came in again, each of them having a bundle of hay in her apron. Hanrahan was not singing now, but he was talking to Oona very fast and soft, and he was saying: 'The house is narrow but the world is wide, and there is no true lover that need be afraid of night or morning or sun or stars or shadows of evening, or any earthly thing.' 'Hanrahan,' said the mother then, striking him on the shoulder, 'will you give me a hand here for a minute?' 'Do that, Hanrahan,' said the woman of the neighbours, 'and help us to make this hay into a rope, for you are ready with your hands, and a blast of wind has loosened the thatch on the haystack.'

'I will do that for you,' said he, and he took the little stick in his hands, and the mother began giving out the hay, and he twisting it, but he was hurrying to have done with it, and to be free again. The women went on talking and giving out the hay, and encouraging him, and saying what a good twister of a rope he was, better than their own neighbours or than anyone they had ever seen. And Hanrahan saw that Oona was watching him, and he began to twist very quick and with his head high, and to boast of the readiness of his hands, and the learning he had in his head, and the strength in his arms. And as he was boasting, he went backward, twisting the rope always till he came to the door that was open behind him, and without thinking he passed the threshold and was out on the road. And no sooner was he there than the mother made a sudden rush, and threw out the rope after him, and she shut the door and the half-door and put a bolt upon them.

She was well pleased when she had done that, and laughed out loud, and the neighbours laughed and praised her. But they heard him beating at the door, and saying words of cursing outside it, and the mother had but time to stop Oona that had her hand upon the bolt to open it. She made a sign to the fiddler then, and he began a reel, and one of the young men asked no leave but caught hold of Oona and brought her into the thick of the dance. And when it was over and the fiddle had stopped, there was no sound at all of anything outside, but the road was as quiet as before.

As to Hanrahan, when he knew he was shut out and that there was neither shelter nor drink nor a girl's ear for him that night, the anger and the courage went out of him, and he went on to where the waves were beating on the strand.

He sat down on a big stone, and he began swinging his right arm and singing slowly to himself, the way he did always to hearten himself when every other thing failed him. And whether it was that time or another time he made the song that is called to this day 'The Twisting of the Rope,' and that begins, 'What was the dead cat that put me in this place,' is not known.

But after he had been singing awhile, mist and shadows seemed to gather about him, sometimes coming out of the sea, and sometimes moving upon it. It seemed to him that one of the shadows was the queen-woman he had seen in her sleep at Slieve Echtge; not in her sleep now, but mocking, and calling out to them that were behind her: 'He was weak, he was weak, he had no courage.' And he felt the strands of the rope in his hand yet, and went on twisting it, but it seemed to him as he twisted, that it had all the sorrows of the world in it. And then it seemed to him as if the rope had changed in his dream into a great water-worm that came out of the sea, and that twisted itself about him, and held him closer and closer, and grew from big to bigger till the whole of the earth and skies were wound up in it, and the stars themselves were but the shining of the ridges of its skin. And then he got free of it, and went on, shaking and unsteady, along the edge of the strand, and the grey shapes were flying here and there around him. And this is what they were saying, 'It is a pity for him that refuses the call of the daughters of the Sidhe, for he will find no comfort in the love of the women of the earth to the end of life and time, and the cold of the grave is in his heart for ever. It is death he has chosen; let him die, let him die, let him die.'

HANRAHAN AND CATHLEEN THE DAUGHTER OF HOOLIHAN.

It was travelling northward Hanrahan was one time, giving a hand to a farmer now and again in the hurried time of the year, and telling his stories and making his share of songs at wakes and at weddings.

He chanced one day to overtake on the road to Collooney one Margaret Rooney, a woman he used to know in Munster when he was a young man. She had no good name at that time, and it was the priest routed her out of the place at last. He knew her by her walk and by the colour of her eyes, and by a way she had of putting back the hair off her face with her left hand. She had been wandering about, she said, selling herrings and the like, and now she was going back to Sligo, to the place in the Burrough where she was living with another woman, Mary Gillis, who had much the same story as herself. She would be well pleased, she said, if he would come and stop in the house with them, and be singing his songs to the bacachs and blind men and fiddlers of the Burrough. She remembered him well, she said, and had a wish for him; and as to Mary Gillis, she had some of his songs off by heart, so he need not be afraid of not getting good treatment, and all the bacachs and poor men that heard him would give him a share of their own earnings for his stories and his songs while he was with them, and would carry his name into all the parishes of Ireland.

He was glad enough to go with her, and to find a woman to be listening to the story of his troubles and to be comforting him. It was at the moment of the fall of day when every man may pass as handsome and every woman as comely. She put her arm about him when he told her of the misfortune of the Twisting of the Rope, and in the half light she looked as well as another.

They kept in talk all the way to the Burrough, and as for Mary Gillis, when she saw him and heard who he was, she went near crying to think of having a man with so great a name in the house.

Hanrahan was well pleased to settle down with them for a while, for he was tired with wandering; and since the day he found the little cabin fallen in, and Mary Lavelle gone from it, and the thatch scattered, he had never asked to have any place of his own; and he had never stopped long enough in any place to see the green leaves come where he had seen the old leaves wither, or to see the wheat harvested where he had seen it sown. It was a good change to him to have shelter from the wet, and a fire in the evening time, and his share of food put on the table without the asking.

He made a good many of his songs while he was living there, so well cared for and so quiet, The most of them were love songs, but some were songs of repentance, and some were songs about Ireland and her griefs, under one name or another.

Every evening the bacachs and beggars and blind men and fiddlers would gather into the house and listen to his songs and his poems, and his stories about the old time of the Fianna, and they kept them in their memories that were never spoiled with books; and so they brought his name to every wake and wedding and pattern in the whole of Connaught. He was never so well off or made so much of as he was at that time.

One evening of December he was singing a little song that he said he had heard from the green plover of the mountain, about the fair-haired boys that had left Limerick, and that were wandering and going astray in all parts of the world. There were a good many people in the room that night, and two or three little lads that had crept in, and sat on the floor near the fire, and were too busy with the roasting of a potato in the ashes or some such thing to take much notice of him; but they remembered long afterwards when his name had gone up, the sound of his voice, and what way he had moved his hand, and the look of him as he sat on the edge of the bed, with his shadow falling on the whitewashed wall behind him, and as he moved going up as high as the thatch. And they knew then that they had looked upon a king of the poets of the Gael, and a maker of the dreams of men.

Of a sudden his singing stopped, and his eyes grew misty as if he was looking at some far thing.

Mary Gillis was pouring whiskey into a mug that stood on a table beside him, and she left off pouring and said, 'Is it of leaving us you are thinking?'

Margaret Rooney heard what she said, and did not know why she said it, and she took the words too much in earnest and came over to him, and there was dread in her heart that she was going to lose so wonderful a poet and so good a comrade, and a man that was thought so much of, and that brought so many to her house.

'You would not go away from us, my heart?' she said, catching him by the hand.

'It is not of that I am thinking,' he said, 'but of Ireland and the weight of grief that is on her.' And he leaned his head against his hand, and began to sing these words, and the sound of his voice was like the wind in a lonely place.

> The old brown thorn trees break in two high over Cummen Strand
> Under a bitter black wind that blows from the left hand;
> Our courage breaks like an old tree in a black wind and dies,
> But we have hidden in our hearts the flame out of the eyes
> Of Cathleen the daughter of Hoolihan.
>
> The winds was bundled up the clouds high over Knocknarea
> And thrown the thunder on the stones for all that Maeve can say;
> Angers that are like noisy clouds have set our hearts abeat,
> But we have all bent low and low and kissed the quiet feet
> Of Cathleen the daughter of Hoolihan.
>
> The yellow pool has overflowed high upon Clooth-na-Bare,
> For the wet winds are blowing out of the clinging air;
> Like heavy flooded waters our bodies and our blood,
> But purer than a tall candle before the Holy Rood
> Is Cathleen the daughter of Hoolihan.

While he was singing, his voice began to break, and tears came rolling down his cheeks, and Margaret Rooney put down her face into her hands and began to cry along with him. Then a blind beggar by the fire shook his rags with a sob, and after that there was no one of them all but cried tears down.

RED HANRAHAN'S CURSE.

One fine May morning a long time after Hanrahan had left Margaret Rooney's house, he was walking the road near Collooney, and the sound of the birds singing in the bushes that were white with blossom set him singing as he went. It was to his own little place he was going, that was no more than a cabin, but that pleased him well. For he was tired of so many years of wandering from shelter to shelter at all times of the year, and although he was seldom refused a welcome and a share of what was in the house, it seemed to him sometimes that his mind was getting stiff like his joints, and it was not so easy to him as it used to be to make fun and sport through the night, and to set all the boys laughing with his pleasant talk, and to coax the women with his songs. And a while ago, he had turned into a cabin that some poor man had left to go harvesting and had never come to again. And when he had mended the thatch and made a bed in the corner with a few sacks and bushes, and had swept out the floor, he was well content to have a little place for himself, where he could go in and out as he liked, and put his head in his hands through the length of an evening if the fret was on him, and loneliness after the old times. One by one the neighbours began to send their children in to get some learning from him, and with what they brought, a few eggs or an oaten cake or a couple of sods of turf, he made out a way of living. And if he went for a wild day and night now and again to the Burrough, no one would say a word, knowing him to be a poet, with wandering in his heart.

It was from the Burrough he was coming that May morning, light-hearted enough, and singing some new song that had come to him. But it was not long till a hare ran across his path, and made away into the fields, through the loose stones of the wall. And he knew it was no good sign a hare to have crossed his path, and he remembered the hare that had led him away to Slieve Echtge the time Mary

Lavelle was waiting for him, and how he had never known content for any length of time since then. 'And it is likely enough they are putting some bad thing before me now,' he said.

And after he said that he heard the sound of crying in the field beside him, and he looked over the wall. And there he saw a young girl sitting under a bush of white hawthorn, and crying as if her heart would break. Her face was hidden in her hands, but her soft hair and her white neck and the young look of her, put him in mind of Bridget Purcell and Margaret Gillane and Maeve Connelan and Oona Curry and Celia Driscoll, and the rest of the girls he had made songs for and had coaxed the heart from with his flattering tongue.

She looked up, and he saw her to be a girl of the neighbours, a farmer's daughter. 'What is on you, Nora?' he said. 'Nothing you could take from me, Red Hanrahan.' 'If there is any sorrow on you it is I myself should be well able to serve you,' he said then, 'for it is I know the history of the Greeks, and I know well what sorrow is and parting, and the hardship of the world. And if I am not able to save you from trouble,' he said, 'there is many a one I have saved from it with the power that is in my songs, as it was in the songs of the poets that were before me from the beginning of the world. And it is with the rest of the poets I myself will be sitting and talking in some far place beyond the world, to the end of life and time,' he said. The girl stopped her crying, and she said, 'Owen Hanrahan, I often heard you have had sorrow and persecution, and that you know all the troubles of the world since the time you refused your love to the queen-woman in Slieve Echtge; and that she never left you in quiet since. But when it is people of this earth that have harmed you, it is yourself knows well the way to put harm on them again. And will you do now what I ask you, Owen Hanrahan?' she said. 'I will do that indeed,' said he.

'It is my father and my mother and my brothers,' she said, 'that are marrying me to old Paddy Doe, because he has a farm of a hundred acres under the mountain. And it is what you can do, Hanrahan,' she said, 'put him into a rhyme the same way you put old Peter Kilmartin in one the time you were young, that sorrow may be over him rising up and lying down, that will put him thinking of Collooney churchyard and not of marriage. And let you make no delay about it, for it is for to-morrow they have the marriage settled, and I would sooner see the sun rise on the day of my death than on that day.'

'I will put him into a song that will bring shame and sorrow over him; but tell me how many years has he, for I would put them in the song?'

'O, he has years upon years. He is as old as you yourself, Red Hanrahan.' 'As old as myself,' said Hanrahan, and his voice was as if broken; 'as old as myself; there are twenty years and more between us! It is a bad day indeed for Owen Hanrahan when a young girl with the blossom of May in her cheeks thinks him to be an old man. And my grief!' he said, 'you have put a thorn in my heart.'

He turned from her then and went down the road till he came to a stone, and he sat down on it, for it seemed as if all the weight of the years had come on him in the minute. And he remembered it was not many days ago that a woman in some house had said: 'It is not Red Hanrahan you are now but yellow Hanrahan, for your hair is turned to the colour of a wisp of tow.' And another woman he had asked for a drink had not given him new milk but sour; and sometimes the girls would be whispering and laughing with young ignorant men while he himself was in the middle of giving out his poems or his talk. And he thought of the stiffness of his joints when he first rose of a morning, and the pain of his knees after making a journey, and it seemed to him as if he was come to be a very old man, with cold in the shoulders and speckled shins and his wind breaking and he himself withering away. And with those thoughts there came on him a great anger against old age and all it brought with it. And just then he looked up and saw a great spotted eagle sailing slowly towards Ballygawley, and he cried out: 'You, too, eagle of Ballygawley, are old, and your wings are full of gaps, and I will put you and your ancient comrades, the Pike of Dargan Lake and the Yew of the Steep Place of the Strangers into my rhyme, that there may be a curse on you for ever.'

There was a bush beside him to the left, flowering like the rest, and a little gust of wind blew the white blossoms over his coat. 'May blossoms,' he said, gathering them up in the hollow of his hand, 'you never know age because you die away in your beauty, and I will put you into my rhyme and give you my blessing.'

He rose up then and plucked a little branch from the bush, and carried it in his hand. But it is old and broken he looked going home that day with the stoop in his shoulders and the darkness in his face.

When he got to his cabin there was no one there, and he went and lay down on the bed for a while as he was used to do when he wanted to make a poem or a praise or a curse. And it was not long he was in making it this time, for the power of the curse-making bards was upon him. And when he had made it he searched his mind how he could send it out over the whole countryside.

Some of the scholars began coming in then, to see if there would be any school that day, and Hanrahan rose up and sat on the bench by the hearth, and they all stood around him.

They thought he would bring out the Virgil or the Mass book or the primer, but instead of that he held up the little branch of hawthorn he had in his hand yet. 'Children,' he said, 'this is a new lesson I have for you to-day.

'You yourselves and the beautiful people of the world are like this blossom, and old age is the wind that comes and blows the blossom away. And I have made a curse upon old age and upon the old men, and listen now while I give it out to you.' And this is what he said--

The poet, Owen Hanrahan, under a bush of may
Calls down a curse on his own head because it withers grey;
Then on the speckled eagle cock of Ballygawley Hill,
Because it is the oldest thing that knows of cark and ill;
And on the yew that has been green from the times out of mind
By the Steep Place of the Strangers and the Gap of the Wind;
And on the great grey pike that broods in Castle Dargan Lake
Having in his long body a many a hook and ache;
Then curses he old Paddy Bruen of the Well of Bride
Because no hair is on his head and drowsiness inside.
Then Paddy's neighbour, Peter Hart, and Michael Gill, his friend,
Because their wandering histories are never at an end.
And then old Shemus Cullinan, shepherd of the Green Lands
Because he holds two crutches between his crooked hands;
Then calls a curse from the dark North upon old Paddy Doe,
Who plans to lay his withering head upon a breast of snow,
Who plans to wreck a singing voice and break a merry heart,
He bids a curse hang over him till breath and body part;
But he calls down a blessing on the blossom of the may,

Because it comes in beauty, and in beauty blows away.

He said it over to the children verse by verse till all of them could say a part of it, and some that were the quickest could say the whole of it.

'That will do for to-day,' he said then. 'And what you have to do now is to go out and sing that song for a while, to the tune of the Green Bunch of Rushes, to everyone you meet, and to the old men themselves.'

'I will do that,' said one of the little lads; 'I know old Paddy Doe well. Last Saint John's Eve we dropped a mouse down his chimney, but this is better than a mouse.'

'I will go into the town of Sligo and sing it in the street,' said another of the boys. 'Do that,' said Hanrahan, 'and go into the Burrough and tell it to Margaret Rooney and Mary Gillis, and bid them sing to it, and to make the beggars and the bacachs sing it wherever they go.' The children ran out then, full of pride and of mischief, calling out the song as they ran, and Hanrahan knew there was no danger it would not be heard.

He was sitting outside the door the next morning, looking at his scholars as they came by in twos and threes. They were nearly all come, and he was considering the place of the sun in the heavens to know whether it was time to begin, when he heard a sound that was like the buzzing of a swarm of bees in the air, or the rushing of a hidden river in time of flood. Then he saw a crowd coming up to the cabin from the road, and he took notice that all the crowd was made up of old men, and that the leaders of it were Paddy Bruen, Michael Gill and Paddy Doe, and there was not one in the crowd but had in his hand an ash stick or a blackthorn. As soon as they caught sight of him, the sticks began to wave hither and thither like branches in a storm, and the old feet to run.

He waited no longer, but made off up the hill behind the cabin till he was out of their sight.

After a while he came back round the hill, where he was hidden by the furze growing along a ditch. And when he came in sight of his cabin he saw that all the old men had gathered around it, and one of them was just at that time thrusting a rake with a wisp of lighted straw on it into the thatch.

'My grief,' he said, 'I have set Old Age and Time and Weariness and Sickness against me, and I must go wandering again. And, O Blessed Queen of Heaven,' he said, 'protect me from the Eagle of Ballygawley, the Yew Tree of the Steep Place of the Strangers, the Pike of Castle Dargan Lake, and from the lighted wisps of their kindred, the Old Men!'

HANRAHAN'S VISION.

It was in the month of June Hanrahan was on the road near Sligo, but he did not go into the town, but turned towards Beinn Bulben; for there were thoughts of the old times coming upon him, and he had no mind to meet with common men. And as he walked he was singing to himself a song that had come to him one time in his dreams:

O Death's old bony finger
Will never find us there
In the high hollow townland
Where love's to give and to spare;
Where boughs have fruit and blossom
At all times of the year;
Where rivers are running over
With red beer and brown beer.
An old man plays the bagpipes
In a gold and silver wood;
Queens, their eyes blue like the ice,
Are dancing in a crowd.

The little fox he murmured,
'O what of the world's bane?'
The sun was laughing sweetly,
The moon plucked at my rein;
But the little red fox murmured,
'O do not pluck at his rein,

He is riding to the townland
That is the world's bane.'

When their hearts are so high
That they would come to blows,
They unhook their heavy swords
From golden and silver boughs:
But all that are killed in battle
Awaken to life again:
It is lucky that their story
Is not known among men.
For O, the strong farmers
That would let the spade lie,
Their hearts would be like a cup
That somebody had drunk dry.

Michael will unhook his trumpet
From a bough overhead,
And blow a little noise
When the supper has been spread.
Gabriel will come from the water
With a fish tail, and talk
Of wonders that have happened
On wet roads where men walk,
And lift up an old horn
Of hammered silver, and drink
Till he has fallen asleep
Upon the starry brink.

Hanrahan had begun to climb the mountain then, and he gave over singing, for it was a long climb for him, and every now and again he had to sit down and to rest for a while. And one time he was resting he took notice of a wild briar bush, with blossoms on it, that was growing beside a rath, and it brought to mind the wild roses he used to bring to Mary Lavelle, and to no woman after her. And he tore off a little branch of the bush, that had buds on it and open blossoms, and he went on with his song:

> The little fox he murmured,
> 'O what of the world's bane?'
> The sun was laughing sweetly,
> The moon plucked at my rein;
> But the little red fox murmured,
> 'O do not pluck at his rein,
> He is riding to the townland
> That is the world's bane.'

And he went on climbing the hill, and left the rath, and there came to his mind some of the old poems that told of lovers, good and bad, and of some that were awakened from the sleep of the grave itself by the strength of one another's love, and brought away to a life in some shadowy place, where they are waiting for the judgment and banished from the face of God.

And at last, at the fall of day, he came to the Steep Gap of the Strangers, and there he laid himself down along a ridge of rock, and looked into the valley, that was full of grey mist spreading from mountain to mountain.

And it seemed to him as he looked that the mist changed to shapes of shadowy men and women, and his heart began to beat with the fear and the joy of the sight. And his hands, that were always restless, began to pluck off the leaves of the roses on the little branch, and he watched them as they went floating down into the valley in a little fluttering troop.

Suddenly he heard a faint music, a music that had more laughter in it and more crying than all the music of this world. And his heart rose when he heard that, and he began to laugh out loud, for he knew that music was made by some who had a beauty and a greatness beyond the people of this world. And it seemed to him that the little soft rose leaves as they went fluttering down into the valley began to change their shape till they looked like a troop of men and women far off in the mist, with the colour of the roses on them. And then that colour changed to many colours, and what he saw was a long line of tall beautiful young men, and of queen-women, that were not going from him but coming towards him and past him, and their faces were full of tenderness for all their proud looks, and were very pale and worn, as if they were seeking and ever seeking for high sorrowful things. And shadowy arms were stretched out of the mist as if to take hold of them, but could not touch them, for the quiet that was about them could not be broken. And before them and beyond them, but at a distance as if in reverence, there were other shapes, sinking and rising and coming and going, and Hanrahan knew them by their whirling flight to be the Sidhe, the ancient defeated gods; and the shadowy arms did not rise to take hold of them, for they were of those that can neither sin nor obey. And they all lessened then in the distance, and they seemed to be going towards the white door that is in the side of the mountain.

The mist spread out before him now like a deserted sea washing the mountains with long grey waves, but while he was looking at it, it began to fill again with a flowing broken witless life that was a part of itself, and arms and pale heads covered with tossing hair appeared in the greyness. It rose higher and higher till it was level with the edge of the steep rock, and then the shapes grew to be solid, and a new procession half lost in mist passed very slowly with uneven steps, and in the midst of each shadow there was something shining in the starlight. They came nearer and nearer, and Hanrahan saw that they also were lovers, and that they had heart-shaped mirrors instead of hearts, and they were looking and ever looking on their own faces in one another's mirrors. They passed on, sinking downward as they passed, and other shapes rose in their place, and these did not keep side by side, but followed after one another, holding out wild beckoning arms, and he saw that those who were followed were women, and as to their heads they were beyond all beauty, but as to their bodies they were but shadows without life, and their long hair was moving and trembling about them, as if it lived with some terrible life of its own. And then the mist rose of a sudden and hid them, and then a light gust of wind blew them away towards the north-east, and covered Hanrahan at the same time with a white wing of cloud.

He stood up trembling and was going to turn away from the valley, when he saw two dark and half-hidden forms standing as if in the air just beyond the rock, and one of them that had the sorrowful eyes of a beggar said to him in a woman's voice, 'Speak to me, for no one in this world or any other world has spoken to me for seven hundred years.'

'Tell me who are those that have passed by,' said Hanrahan.

'Those that passed first,' the woman said, 'are the lovers that had the greatest name in the old times, Blanad and Deirdre and Grania and their dear comrades, and a great many that are not so well known but are as well loved. And because it was not only the blossom of youth they were looking for in one another, but the beauty that is as lasting as the night and the stars, the night and the stars hold them for ever from the warring and the perishing, in spite of the wars and the bitterness their love brought into the world. And those that came next,' she said, 'and that still breathe the sweet air and have the mirrors in their hearts, are not put in songs by the poets, because they sought only to triumph one over the other, and so to prove their strength and beauty, and out of this they made a kind of love. And as to the women with shadow-bodies, they desired neither to triumph nor to love but only to be loved, and there is no blood in their hearts or in their bodies until it flows through them from a kiss, and their life is but for a moment. All these are unhappy, but I am the unhappiest of all, for I am Dervadilla, and this is Dermot, and it was our sin brought the Norman into Ireland. And the curses of all the generations are upon us, and none are punished as we are punished. It was but the blossom of the man and of the woman we loved in one another, the dying beauty of the dust and not the everlasting beauty. When we died there was no lasting unbreakable quiet about us, and the bitterness of the battles we brought into Ireland turned to our own punishment. We go wandering together for ever, but Dermot that was my lover sees me always as a body that has been a long time in the ground, and I know that is the way he sees me. Ask me more, ask me more, for all the years have left their wisdom in my heart, and no one has listened to me for seven hundred years.'

A great terror had fallen upon Hanrahan, and lifting his arms above his head he screamed out loud three times, and the cattle in the valley lifted their heads and lowed, and the birds in the wood at the edge of the mountain awaked out of their sleep and fluttered through the trembling leaves. But a little below the edge of the rock, the troop of rose leaves still fluttered in the air, for the gateway of Eternity had opened and shut again in one beat of the heart.

THE DEATH OF HANRAHAN.

Hanrahan, that was never long in one place, was back again among the villages that are at the foot of Slieve Echtge, Illeton and Scalp and Ballylee, stopping sometimes in one house and sometimes in another, and finding a welcome in every place for the sake of the old times and of his poetry and his learning. There was some silver and some copper money in the little leather bag under his coat, but it was seldom he needed to take anything from it, for it was little he used, and there was not one of the people that would have taken payment from him. His hand had grown heavy on the blackthorn he leaned on, and his cheeks were hollow and worn, but so far as food went, potatoes and milk and a bit of oaten cake, he had what he wanted of it; and it is not on the edge of so wild and boggy a place as Echtge a mug of spirits would be wanting, with the taste of the turf smoke on it. He would wander about the big wood at Kinadife, or he would sit through many hours of the day among the rushes about Lake Belshragh, listening to the streams from the hills, or watching the shadows in the brown bog pools; sitting so quiet as not to startle the deer that came down from the heather to the grass and the tilled fields at the fall of night. As the days went by it seemed as if he was beginning to belong to some world out of sight and misty, that has for its mearing the colours that are beyond all other colours and the silences that are beyond all silences of this world. And sometimes he would hear coming and going in the wood music that when it stopped went from his memory like a dream; and once in the stillness of midday he heard a sound like the clashing of many swords, that went on for long time without any break. And at the fall of night and at moonrise the lake would grow to be like a gateway of silver and shining stones, and there would come from its silence the faint sound of keening and of frightened laughter broken by the wind, and many pale beckoning hands.

He was sitting looking into the water one evening in harvest time, thinking of all the secrets that were shut into the lakes and the mountains, when he heard a cry coming from the south, very faint at first, but getting louder and clearer as the shadow of the rushes grew longer, till he could hear the words, 'I am beautiful, I am beautiful; the birds in the air, the moths under the leaves, the flies over the water look at me, for they never saw any one so beautiful as myself. I am young; I am young: look upon me, mountains; look upon me, perishing woods, for my body will shine like the white waters when you have been hurried away. You and the whole race of men, and the race of the beasts and the race of the fish and the winged race are dropping like a candle that is nearly burned out, but I laugh out because I am in my youth.' The voice would break off from time to time, as if tired, and then it would begin again, calling out always the same words, 'I am beautiful, I am beautiful.' Presently the bushes at the edge of the little lake trembled for a moment, and a very old woman forced her way among them, and passed by Hanrahan, walking with very slow steps. Her face was of the colour of earth, and more wrinkled than the face of any old hag that was ever seen, and her grey hair was hanging in wisps, and the rags she was wearing did not hide her dark skin that was roughened by all weathers. She passed by him with her eyes wide open, and her head high, and her arms hanging straight beside her, and she went into the shadow of the hills towards the west.

A sort of dread came over Hanrahan when he saw her, for he knew her to be one Winny Byrne, that went begging from place to place crying always the same cry, and he had often heard that she had once such wisdom that all the women of the neighbours used to go looking for advice from her, and that she had a voice so beautiful that men and women would come from every part to hear her sing at a wake or a wedding; and that the Others, the great Sidhe, had stolen her wits one Samhain night many years ago, when she had fallen asleep on the edge of a rath, and had seen in her dreams the servants of Echtge of the hills.

And as she vanished away up the hillside, it seemed as if her cry, 'I am beautiful, I am beautiful,' was coming from among the stars in the heavens.

There was a cold wind creeping among the rushes, and Hanrahan began to shiver, and he rose up to go to some house where there would be a fire on the hearth. But instead of turning down the hill as he was used, he went on up the hill, along the little track that was maybe a road and maybe the dry bed of a stream. It was the same way Winny had gone, and it led to the little cabin where she stopped when she stopped in any place at all. He walked very slowly up the hill as if he had a great load on his back, and at last he saw a light a little to the left, and he thought it likely it was from Winny's house it was shining, and he turned from the path to go to it. But clouds had come over the sky, and he could not well see his way, and after he had gone a few steps his foot slipped and he fell into a bog drain, and though he dragged himself out of it, holding on to the roots of the heather, the fall had given him a great shake, and he felt better fit to lie down than to go travelling. But he had always great courage, and he made his way on, step by step, till at last he came to Winny's cabin, that had no window, but the light was shining from the door. He thought to go into it and to rest for a while, but when he came to the door he did not see Winny inside it, but what he saw was four old grey-haired women playing cards, but Winny herself was not among them. Hanrahan sat down on a heap of turf beside the door, for he was tired out and out, and had no wish for talking or for card-playing, and his bones and his joints aching the way they were. He could hear the four women talking as they played, and calling out their hands. And it seemed to him that they were saying, like the strange man in the barn long ago: 'Spades and Diamonds, Courage and Power. Clubs and Hearts, Knowledge and Pleasure.' And he went on saying those words over and over to himself; and whether or not he was in his dreams, the pain that was in his shoulder never left him. And after a while the four women in the cabin began to quarrel, and each one to say the other had not played fair, and their voices grew from loud to louder, and their screams and their curses, till at last the whole air was filled with the noise of them around and above the house, and Hanrahan, hearing it between sleep and waking, said: 'That is the sound of the fighting between the friends and the ill-wishers of a man that is near his death. And I wonder,' he said, 'who is the man in this lonely place that is near his death.'

It seemed as if he had been asleep a long time, and he opened his eyes, and the face he saw over him was the old wrinkled face of Winny of the Cross Road. She was looking hard at him, as if to make sure he was not dead, and she wiped away the blood that had grown dry on his face with a wet cloth, and after a while she partly helped him and partly lifted him into the cabin, and laid him down on what served her for a bed. She gave him a couple of potatoes from a pot on the fire, and, what served him better, a mug of spring water. He slept a little now and again, and sometimes he heard her singing to herself as she moved about the house, and so the night wore away. When the sky began to brighten with the dawn he felt for the bag; where his little store of money was, and held it out to her, and she took out a bit of copper and a bit of silver money, but she let it drop again as if it was nothing to her, maybe because it was not money she was used to beg for, but food and rags; or maybe because the rising of the dawn was filling her with pride and a new belief in her own great beauty. She went out and cut a few armfuls of heather, and brought it in and heaped it over Hanrahan, saying something about the cold of the morning, and while she did that he took notice of the wrinkles in her face, and the greyness of her hair, and the broken teeth that were black and full of gaps. And when he was well covered with the heather she went out of the door and away down the side of the mountain, and he could hear her cry, 'I am beautiful, I am beautiful,' getting less and less as she went, till at last it died away altogether.

Hanrahan lay there through the length of the day, in his pains and his weakness, and when the shadows of the evening were falling he heard her voice again coming up the hillside, and she came in and boiled the potatoes and shared them with him the same way as before. And one day after another passed like that, and the weight of his flesh was heavy about him. But little by little as he grew weaker he knew there were some greater than himself in the room with him, and that the house began to be filled with them; and it seemed to him they had all power in their hands, and that they might with one touch of the hand break down the wall the hardness of pain had built about him, and take him into their own world. And sometimes he could hear voices, very faint and joyful, crying from the rafters or out of the flame on the hearth, and other times the whole house was filled with music that went through it like a wind. And after a while his weakness left no place for pain, and there grew up about him a great silence like the silence in the heart of a lake, and there came through it like the flame of a rushlight the faint joyful voices ever and always.

One morning he heard music somewhere outside the door, and as the day passed it grew louder and louder until it drowned the faint joyful voices, and even Winny's cry upon the hillside at the fall of evening. About midnight and in a moment, the walls seemed to melt away and to leave his bed floating on a pale misty light that shone on every side as far as the eye could see; and after the first blinding of his eyes he saw that it was full of great shadowy figures rushing here and there.

At the same time the music came very clearly to him, and he knew that it was but the continual clashing of swords.

'I am after my death,' he said, 'and in the very heart of the music of Heaven. O Cheruhim and Seraphim, receive my soul!'

At his cry the light where it was nearest to him filled with sparks of yet brighter light, and he saw that these were the points of swords turned towards his heart; and then a sudden flame, bright and burning like God's love or God's hate, swept over the light and went out and he was in darkness. At first he could see nothing, for all was as dark as if there was black bog earth about him, but all of a sudden the fire blazed up as if a wisp of straw had been thrown upon it. And as he looked at it, the light was shining on the big pot that was hanging from a hook, and on the flat stone where Winny used to bake a cake now and again, and on the long rusty knife she used to be cutting the roots of the heather with, and on the long blackthorn stick he had brought into the house himself. And when he saw those four things, some memory came into Hanrahan's mind, and strength came back to him, and he rose sitting up in the bed, and he said very loud and clear: 'The Cauldron, the Stone, the Sword, the Spear. What are they? Who do they belong to? And I have asked the question this time,' he said.

And then he fell back again, weak, and the breath going from him.

Winny Byrne, that had been tending the fire, came over then, having her eyes fixed on the bed; and the faint laughing voices began crying out again, and a pale light, grey like a wave, came creeping over the room, and he did not know from what secret world it came. He saw Winny's withered face and her withered arms that were grey like crumbled earth, and weak as he was he shrank back farther towards the wall. And then there came out of the mud-stiffened rags arms as white and as shadowy as the foam on a river, and they were put about his body, and a voice that he could hear well but that seemed to come from a long way off said to him in a whisper: 'You will go looking for me no more upon the breasts of women.'

'Who are you?' he said then.

'I am one of the lasting people, of the lasting unwearied Voices, that make my dwelling in the broken and the dying, and those that have lost their wits; and I came looking for you, and you are mine until the whole world is burned out like a candle that is spent. And look up now,' she said, 'for the wisps that are for our wedding are lighted.'

He saw then that the house was crowded with pale shadowy hands, and that every hand was holding what was sometimes like a wisp lighted for a marriage, and sometimes like a tall white candle for the dead.

When the sun rose on the morning of the morrow Winny of the Cross Roads rose up from where she was sitting beside the body, and began her begging from townland to townland, singing the same song as she walked, 'I am beautiful, I am beautiful. The birds in the air, the moths under the leaves, the flies over the water look at me. Look at me, perishing woods, for my body will be shining like the lake water after you have been hurried away. You and the old race of men, and the race of the beasts, and the race of the fish, and the winged race, are wearing away like a candle that has been burned out. But I laugh out loud, because I am in my youth.'

She did not come back that night or any night to the cabin, and it was not till the end of two days that the turf cutters going to the bog found the body of Red Owen Hanrahan, and gathered men to wake him and women to keen him, and gave him a burying worthy of so great a poet.

The Codes Of Hammurabi And Moses
W. W. Davies

QTY

The discovery of the Hammurabi Code is one of the greatest achievements of archaeology, and is of paramount interest, not only to the student of the Bible, but also to all those interested in ancient history...

Religion ISBN: *1-59462-338-4*

Pages:132
MSRP $12.95

The Theory of Moral Sentiments
Adam Smith

QTY

This work from 1749. contains original theories of conscience amd moral judgment and it is the foundation for systemof morals.

Philosophy ISBN: *1-59462-777-0*

Pages:536
MSRP $19.95

Jessica's First Prayer
Hesba Stretton

QTY

In a screened and secluded corner of one of the many railway-bridges which span the streets of London there could be seen a few years ago, from five o'clock every morning until half past eight, a tidily set-out coffee-stall, consisting of a trestle and board, upon which stood two large tin cans, with a small fire of charcoal burning under each so as to keep the coffee boiling during the early hours of the morning when the work-people were thronging into the city on their way to their daily toil...

Childrens ISBN: *1-59462-373-2*

Pages:84
MSRP $9.95

My Life and Work
Henry Ford

QTY

Henry Ford revolutionized the world with his implementation of mass production for the Model T automobile. Gain valuable business insight into his life and work with his own auto-biography... "We have only started on our development of our country we have not as yet, with all our talk of wonderful progress, done more than scratch the surface. The progress has been wonderful enough but..."

Biographies/ ISBN: *1-59462-198-5*

Pages:300
MSRP $21.95

The Art of Cross-Examination
Francis Wellman

QTY

I presume it is the experience of every author, after his first book is published upon an important subject, to be almost overwhelmed with a wealth of ideas and illustrations which could readily have been included in his book, and which to his own mind, at least, seem to make a second edition inevitable. Such certainly was the case with me; and when the first edition had reached its sixth impression in five months, I rejoiced to learn that it seemed to my publishers that the book had met with a sufficiently favorable reception to justify a second and considerably enlarged edition. ..

Reference   ISBN: *1-59462-647-2*

Pages:412

MSRP $19.95

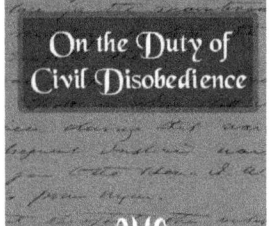

On the Duty of Civil Disobedience
Henry David Thoreau

QTY

Thoreau wrote his famous essay, On the Duty of Civil Disobedience, as a protest against an unjust but popular war and the immoral but popular institution of slave-owning. He did more than write—he declined to pay his taxes, and was hauled off to gaol in consequence. Who can say how much this refusal of his hastened the end of the war and of slavery ?

Law   ISBN: *1-59462-747-9*

Pages:48

MSRP $7.45

Dream Psychology Psychoanalysis for Beginners
Sigmund Freud

QTY

Sigmund Freud, born Sigismund Schlomo Freud (May 6, 1856 - September 23, 1939), was a Jewish-Austrian neurologist and psychiatrist who co-founded the psychoanalytic school of psychology. Freud is best known for his theories of the unconscious mind, especially involving the mechanism of repression; his redefinition of sexual desire as mobile and directed towards a wide variety of objects; and his therapeutic techniques, especially his understanding of transference in the therapeutic relationship and the presumed value of dreams as sources of insight into unconscious desires.

Psychology   ISBN: *1-59462-905-6*

Pages:196

MSRP $15.45

The Miracle of Right Thought
Orison Swett Marden

QTY

Believe with all of your heart that you will do what you were made to do. When the mind has once formed the habit of holding cheerful, happy, prosperous pictures, it will not be easy to form the opposite habit. It does not matter how improbable or how far away this realization may see, or how dark the prospects may be, if we visualize them as best we can, as vividly as possible, hold tenaciously to them and vigorously struggle to attain them, they will gradually become actualized, realized in the life. But a desire, a longing without endeavor, a yearning abandoned or held indifferently will vanish without realization.

Self Help   ISBN: *1-59462-644-8*

Pages:360

MSRP $25.45

www.**bookjungle**.com *email: sales@bookjungle.com fax: 630-214-0564 mail: Book Jungle PO Box 2226 Champaign, IL 61825*

QTY

☐ **The Rosicrucian Cosmo-Conception Mystic Christianity** *by Max Heindel*　ISBN: *1-59462-188-8*　**$38.95**
The Rosicrucian Cosmo-conception is not dogmatic, neither does it appeal to any other authority than the reason of the student. It is: not controversial, but is: sent forth in the, hope that it may help to clear...　New Age/Religion Pages 646

☐ **Abandonment To Divine Providence** *by Jean-Pierre de Caussade*　ISBN: *1-59462-228-0*　**$25.95**
"The Rev. Jean Pierre de Caussade was one of the most remarkable spiritual writers of the Society of Jesus in France in the 18th Century. His death took place at Toulouse in 1751. His works have gone through many editions and have been republished...　Inspirational/Religion Pages 400

☐ **Mental Chemistry** *by Charles Haanel*　ISBN: *1-59462-192-6*　**$23.95**
Mental Chemistry allows the change of material conditions by combining and appropriately utilizing the power of the mind. Much like applied chemistry creates something new and unique out of careful combinations of chemicals the mastery of mental chemistry...　New Age Pages 354

☐ **The Letters of Robert Browning and Elizabeth Barret Barrett 1845-1846 vol II**　ISBN: *1-59462-193-4*　**$35.95**
by Robert Browning and Elizabeth Barrett　Biographies Pages 596

☐ **Gleanings In Genesis (volume I)** *by Arthur W. Pink*　ISBN: *1-59462-130-6*　**$27.45**
Appropriately has Genesis been termed "the seed plot of the Bible" for in it we have, in germ form, almost all of the great doctrines which are afterwards fully developed in the books of Scripture which follow...　Religion/Inspirational Pages 420

☐ **The Master Key** *by L. W. de Laurence*　ISBN: *1-59462-001-6*　**$30.95**
In no branch of human knowledge has there been a more lively increase of the spirit of research during the past few years than in the study of Psychology, Concentration and Mental Discipline. The requests for authentic lessons in Thought Control, Mental Discipline and...　New Age/Business Pages 422

☐ **The Lesser Key Of Solomon Goetia** *by L. W. de Laurence*　ISBN: *1-59462-092-X*　**$9.95**
This translation of the first book of the "Lernegton" which is now for the first time made accessible to students of Talismanic Magic was done, after careful collation and edition, from numerous Ancient Manuscripts in Hebrew, Latin, and French...　New Age/Occult Pages 92

☐ **Rubaiyat Of Omar Khayyam** *by Edward Fitzgerald*　ISBN:*1-59462-332-5*　**$13.95**
Edward Fitzgerald, whom the world has already learned, in spite of his own efforts to remain within the shadow of anonymity, to look upon as one of the rarest poets of the century, was born at Bredfield, in Suffolk, on the 31st of March, 1809. He was the third son of John Purcell...　Music Pages 172

☐ **Ancient Law** *by Henry Maine*　ISBN: *1-59462-128-4*　**$29.95**
The chief object of the following pages is to indicate some of the earliest ideas of mankind, as they are reflected in Ancient Law, and to point out the relation of those ideas to modern thought.　Religion/History Pages 452

☐ **Far-Away Stories** *by William J. Locke*　ISBN: *1-59462-129-2*　**$19.45**
"Good wine needs no bush, but a collection of mixed vintages does. And this book is just such a collection. Some of the stories I do not want to remain buried for ever in the museum files of dead magazine-numbers an author's not unpardonable vanity..."　Fiction Pages 272

☐ **Life of David Crockett** *by David Crockett*　ISBN: *1-59462-250-7*　**$27.45**
"Colonel David Crockett was one of the most remarkable men of the times in which he lived. Born in humble life, but gifted with a strong will, an indomitable courage, and unremitting perseverance...　Biographies/New Age Pages 424

☐ **Lip-Reading** *by Edward Nitchie*　ISBN: *1-59462-206-X*　**$25.95**
Edward B. Nitchie, founder of the New York School for the Hard of Hearing, now the Nitchie School of Lip-Reading, Inc, wrote "LIP-READING Principles and Practice". The development and perfecting of this meritorious work on lip-reading was an undertaking...　How-to Pages 400

☐ **A Handbook of Suggestive Therapeutics, Applied Hypnotism, Psychic Science**　ISBN: *1-59462-214-0*　**$24.95**
by Henry Munro　Health/New Age/Health/Self-help Pages 376

☐ **A Doll's House: and Two Other Plays** *by Henrik Ibsen*　ISBN: *1-59462-112-8*　**$19.95**
Henrik Ibsen created this classic when in revolutionary 1848 Rome. Introducing some striking concepts in playwriting for the realist genre, this play has been studied the world over.　Fiction/Classics/Plays 308

☐ **The Light of Asia** *by sir Edwin Arnold*　ISBN: *1-59462-204-3*　**$13.95**
In this poetic masterpiece, Edwin Arnold describes the life and teachings of Buddha. The man who was to become known as Buddha to the world was born as Prince Gautama of India but he rejected the worldly riches and abandoned the reigns of power when...　Religion/History/Biographies Pages 170

☐ **The Complete Works of Guy de Maupassant** *by Guy de Maupassant*　ISBN: *1-59462-157-8*　**$16.95**
"For days and days, nights and nights, I had dreamed of that first kiss which was to consecrate our engagement, and I knew not on what spot I should put my lips..."　Fiction/Classics Pages 240

☐ **The Art of Cross-Examination** *by Francis L. Wellman*　ISBN: *1-59462-309-0*　**$26.95**
Written by a renowned trial lawyer, Wellman imparts his experience and uses case studies to explain how to use psychology to extract desired information through questioning.　How-to/Science/Reference Pages 408

☐ **Answered or Unanswered?** *by Louisa Vaughan*　ISBN: *1-59462-248-5*　**$10.95**
Miracles of Faith in China　Religion Pages 112

☐ **The Edinburgh Lectures on Mental Science (1909)** *by Thomas*　ISBN: *1-59462-008-3*　**$11.95**
This book contains the substance of a course of lectures recently given by the writer in the Queen Street Hall, Edinburgh. Its purpose is to indicate the Natural Principles governing the relation between Mental Action and Material Conditions...　New Age/Psychology Pages 148

☐ **Ayesha** *by H. Rider Haggard*　ISBN: *1-59462-301-5*　**$24.95**
Verily and indeed it is the unexpected that happens! Probably if there was one person upon the earth from whom the Editor of this, and of a certain previous history, did not expect to hear again...　Classics Pages 380

☐ **Ayala's Angel** *by Anthony Trollope*　ISBN: *1-59462-352-X*　**$29.95**
The two girls were both pretty, but Lucy who was twenty-one who supposed to be simple and comparatively unattractive, whereas Ayala was credited, as her Bombwhat romantic name might show, with poetic charm and a taste for romance. Ayala when her father died was nineteen...　Fiction Pages 484

☐ **The American Commonwealth** *by James Bryce*　ISBN: *1-59462-286-8*　**$34.45**
An interpretation of American democratic political theory. It examines political mechanics and society from the perspective of Scotsman James Bryce　Politics Pages 572

☐ **Stories of the Pilgrims** *by Margaret P. Pumphrey*　ISBN: *1-59462-116-0*　**$17.95**
This book explores pilgrims religious oppression in England as well as their escape to Holland and eventual crossing to America on the Mayflower, and their early days in New England...　History Pages 268

QTY

The Fasting Cure *by Sinclair Upton*   ISBN: *1-59462-222-1* **$13.95** ☐

In the Cosmopolitan Magazine for May, 1910, and in the Contemporary Review (London) for April, 1910, I published an article dealing with my experiences in fasting. I have written a great many magazine articles, but never one which attracted so much attention... New Age/Self Help/Health Pages 164

Hebrew Astrology *by Sepharial*   ISBN: *1-59462-308-2* **$13.45** ☐

In these days of advanced thinking it is a matter of common observation that we have left many of the old landmarks behind and that we are now pressing forward to greater heights and to a wider horizon than that which represented the mind-content of our progenitors... Astrology Pages 144

Thought Vibration or The Law of Attraction in the Thought World   ISBN: *1-59462-127-6* **$12.95** ☐

by William Walker Atkinson   Psychology/Religion Pages 144

Optimism *by Helen Keller*   ISBN: *1-59462-108-X* **$15.95** ☐

Helen Keller was blind, deaf, and mute since 19 months old, yet famously learned how to overcome these handicaps, communicate with the world, and spread her lectures promoting optimism. An inspiring read for everyone... Biographies/Inspirational Pages 84

Sara Crewe *by Frances Burnett*   ISBN: *1-59462-360-0* **$9.45** ☐

In the first place, Miss Minchin lived in London. Her home was a large, dull, tall one, in a large, dull square, where all the houses were alike, and all the sparrows were alike, and where all the door-knockers made the same heavy sound... Childrens/Classic Pages 88

The Autobiography of Benjamin Franklin *by Benjamin Franklin*   ISBN: *1-59462-135-7* **$24.95** ☐

The Autobiography of Benjamin Franklin has probably been more extensively read than any other American historical work, and no other book of its kind has had such ups and downs of fortune. Franklin lived for many years in England, where he was agent... Biographies/History Pages 332

Name	
Email	
Telephone	
Address	
City, State ZIP	

☐ Credit Card   ☐ Check / Money Order

Credit Card Number	
Expiration Date	
Signature	

Please Mail to: Book Jungle
PO Box 2226
Champaign, IL 61825
or Fax to: 630-214-0564

ORDERING INFORMATION

web: *www.bookjungle.com*
email: *sales@bookjungle.com*
fax: *630-214-0564*
mail: *Book Jungle PO Box 2226 Champaign, IL 61825*
or PayPal *to sales@bookjungle.com*

Please contact us for bulk discounts

DIRECT-ORDER TERMS

**20% Discount if You Order
Two or More Books**
Free Domestic Shipping!
Accepted: Master Card, Visa,
Discover, American Express

www.ingramcontent.com/pod-product-compliance
Lightning Source LLC
Chambersburg PA
CBHW081203170626
46813CB00009B/3309